LIFE JOURNEYS IN TIME POETRY	June 21 2019	
Poems by Author are about, family, friends, strangers, places, love, life, death, religion. She writes poems based on her Southern Alabama, Northern New York experience and other poems that come to her mind. The writer work is to uplift the readers and listeners, bring awareness to behavior, human connections. The writer poems seek to bring descriptive, visionary experience to the mind as if you were there. She likes to captivate the readers and listeners emotions and give them something to feel, learn, respect. The poems bring attention to on Present, Being, Higher Energy, Love and Relationship they are essential to life. Know laughter, crazy funny stuff is in this book. What would living be like without funny? These poems were written to share with readers, listeners and to open minds they are meant for all to enjoy.	JOURNEYS IN TIME	

BOOK WRITTEN BY DEBRA J DIXON

LIFE JOURNEY IN TIME-JOURNEYS IN TIME

Poems written overtime

Author Debra J Dixon

INSIDE CREATORS POETRY https://debrajdixon.com

KDP Edition, EDITED BY DEBRA J DIXON

Book Cover Photograph by Debra Dixon June 29,2016

DEDICATION

This dedication is for all those wonderful people I have
built lasting relationships with my parents, daughter,
siblings, other family, friends, teachers and professors
who believe in me and encourage me to be the best at
all I do. I thank Ms. Oprah Winfrey and Mr. Deepak
Chopra for making Meditation available to me and
helping me bring more awareness to the nature of my
Being, motivating me to get up claim my person, goals
and for other opportunities extended. Thanks to two
wonderful Poetry College English Professors for
teaching me and cheering me on Melinda Goodman,
Tracey Morris in New York City. Thanks to my sister,
Joyce Dixon for always motivating me to write my
poems, believing in me and giving me her support, to
Amazon KDP Owners and Staff for making it possible
for me to publish my work. Hunter College, Poetry
Organization, Cave Canem and MODPO, thank you,
for teaching, informing, contacting, including me to
participate, to be a part of the many programs you
offer. My daily thanks to God for my Being, and for
all of our Being on Earth.
Thank you.

Debra J Dixon

CONTENTS

Poems-Journeys In Time

A MAN TO KNOW

Hey Mister!
You know you are a man that is loved.
You know you are a man that is strong.
You know you are a man with created
life and uncreative life.
You are a man with qualities earned
and qualities constantly given to you
from God. God is first, others come in
the order you place them, no one man
has that power over you. You stand
tall posture like a stallion made for
a Race. A respectful man with a stern
face. A completion brown full of
radiance with remarkable traces. A
smile with handsome white teeth
lights up a dark room full of people
in any giving place. You are the
wonderful son to your parents, a
husband to your wife moving
about the place, a Daddy waiting
for the growth of his children,
seeing them get to life
given place, you pray for them
to have better and easier means
down their path and be successful.
You are a brother to your siblings
with their up and down attitudes.
They still make you wonder where
did they come from because their
heads appear to shrink and
sometime you wonder if they
are really Daddy and Mom
child. Perhaps they flew through
windows with Purple feet Aliens
from out space or something
strange as those siblings are,
their loving family, a gift from

God. You are a working man
seeing many strangers all day,
sometime you pick up people
with no dreams. Most of the
time you drive, ride with load
of dreamers and in the load
there are many I am sure is
sure to fulfill their destiny.
You don't know some time
when you are driving and
riding, may be fast or slow
but when you are driven you
just go and arrive. I sat
amongst your load and watch
you cunningly control your
surrounding and you appear
to be a warrior.
I would always like to see.
I imagined you with muscle
rounded off body standing
tall upright, with a shield
against your chest and
holding in your right hand
a heroic Spear as a Warrior.
You are a man indeed
Anyone can clearly see.
You have a persona of a
strong man.
You are a man to Know.

BLAME

Guess who showed up today! Pointing fingers at
Everyone in the universe and everything, it's was
that old Blame! Yes Blame, yes Blame carrying a
Torch with heavy burning flames ready to set
anyone on fire that comes its way. Blame thinks
the universe is why it's so shatter, scatters, cold
and negative. Blame can't find comfort sharing
the universe with no one, everyone is the reason
for Blame problems. Blame always shouts out it's
Your fault! Blame doesn't even know anyone.
Blame your old self need to put your torch flames
out throw it away. Old Blame! Blame accept
yourself as a positive part of the universe stop
bothering others and stop trying to torment us.
Blame no one is bothering you. Blame clear your
Brain become one with the universe with the rest
of us, we are waiting for you to change your ways
and name, you will be just fine. Go on ahead with
your low self-esteem it's not working for you Blame!

REVIEW YOUR VOWS

After being caught by your
Spouse with your lover(s)
has mending been easy after
tossing out the Lover(s)?
Are you and spouse
ending your marriage union?
Now what will you both do?
Continue to be faithful for
the rest of your lives together
or tear one another a part.
Life is too short to live with
regret, wanting what will
never be. If a final note should
go with your marriage let it be
your Vows. If a finally note
should go against your
marriage let it be the opposite
of your vows, a divorce. One
traditional Vow, Will you,
----Have, ----to be your
wife/husband? Will you
Love her/him as long,
as you both shall live? "
("I will").
Let the Divorce be the last
Result Divorce is not in
your Vows. ("I will").

AT THE SKI LODGE

We all had went on
weekend trip up in
New York Catskill
Mountains.
We were all friends of
Friends from New York
area better yet from
Boogie down Bronx and
Harlem's, New York City.
The bus leaves right after
Work Friday, we all come
with our weekend bags
loading our things and
selves on the bus, for
some reason all I could
hear were Marvin Gaye's
records, Let's Get It On
kept playing in my head.
We were a group that
love to party. Anytime
you say party on the
Weekend to us we
threw our hand in the
air and was ready to
party like we just
didn't care. We would
go anywhere that was
clean cut and clear of
danger zones, that's
the way we liked.
We all had got comfortable
on the Bus listening to the
Boom Box up in front of the
Bus, disco and slow jam
Music leading us into
Catskills Mountains of
New York, the party was

On! You saw brothers and
sister so happy. On Friday
night happy, to be going
together somewhere for
the weekend. We drink
that RUM! And
COLA! we couldn't
hang without it back
in the Day! Marvin
Let's Get It On came
on. I became a Female
Marvin singing his
Song, I had my little
drink and I was hitting
those lyrics and then
my Friend Vera said'
you be quiet with your
big old bubble eyes and
let me Sing she had her
some vodka and she
couldn't sing, she
couldn't sing. I said, you
go ahead steal the show
and plus you have bigger
bubble eyes then mine,
she said really!
She started to sing
and we all start
cracking up we who
knew her well
knew she could not
sing but other
didn't have a clue.
She started to sing
Marvin Let's Get It on,
yawl, she
sound like an Opera
Singer with a sore
throat. Vera and their

groups were a little
older in age then our
group, so respect was
in the house. Instead us
saying, Got damn what
the Hell was that, we all
said, man! Oh man! We
can't take no more. She
said, then that Old Debra
better not sing no more.
I said," if all it take for you
not to sing is for me to
stop, on this bus, I will not
utter another" word we
all laugh. We all were
laid back, relaxing,
enjoying the ride. Then
the girl from the third
seat from the Front with
the dark shades started
to yell, leave me alone!
Everyone started
staring and were saying
What's going on? She
and her Man was sitting
together, she yell, he
slapped me again!
They were relatives
of the people sponsoring
the Bus Trip. They said,
everyone go back to
enjoying the ride we will
handle it. Everyone went
back to enjoying them-
selves whispering, one of
the girls said, "Child her
lips were swollen when
she got on the bus and
her eyes was Black and

Blue that's why she's
was wearing them dark
shades at night. That
boy going to kill her ass,
she need have left him
home and stay there
with him." We kept
hearing oh child about
the couple up front
for about ten minutes,
then everyone return
back to party mode.
We had to have some
drama because we
were people full of
life worth living. A
party cut was
playing ,we were
about to arrive at
lodge. In my group
there were four
girls to a room, We
had fun we were
hanging out with
everyone. The town
people, people from
other states, we was
enjoying our
weekend escape
from the city.
We all had met
some Young Men
from Philly we were
all over twenty one.
We bounced from
rooms to rooms
then we all became
more acquainted,
relax, entertaining

from our room
where us fine
young women
were. We were in
the room talking,
dancing drinking
and the guys
was trying to Kiss
us and claim us as
their New York
Women.
We kidded around
went swimming in
the pool, playing
Ticktack Toe, Simon
Said and Giant Step
and other cute
little games. As we
kidded around, two
of my girlfriends and
two Philly boys that
came to join us in
the room. They
were cool the flow
of things were cool.
Velma and Angel
were the girls that
join us. We all was
feeling alright and
goofing off and
laughing the
party was on up in
our room. We all
were into each other.
Velma and Angel
shared rooms.
Velma said, Angel will
you go to the room
and get my cigarettes

Angel would leap up
out her chair run cross
swimming pool
up the steps to their
room and bring back
Velma cigarettes we
continue, partying
then ten minutes later
Velma said, Angel could
you go to room and
bring my pocketbook,
Angel leap up from her
seat run back to room.
Then the third time
Velma said, Angel could
you go to the room,
Angel said, wait a
minute Bitch! Hazel
don't live here
anymore, neither does
Mr. and Mrs. Beazley.
(FYI-Hazel were a Maid
on a TV sitcom)
She were cute, funny
and always on the
run). We all were
laughing,
so hard tears was
falling from our
eyes, even Velma
was laughing.
All of us were
wondering when
Angel were going
to stop running
errands for Velma.

COMFORT MY LOVE

Baby I miss you.
When I am up at night
I cannot sleep baby,
I miss you!
When a hard rain comes,
I am home alone, I
want to run and jump in
your arms.
When I am hurting from
life changes, I need some
comforting, I cry out for
you. I want to pick up
the phone and call you.
I miss you still baby.
I know we have parted.
We went our separate
ways.
Baby, I cry for you some
Nights, I can't stop missing
you. I can't fully get you
off my mind. Just because
we made the decision to
part, I never made a
decision to stop loving you.
I wish every day and
every Night I was in your
arms. I remember them
feeling comforting, warm.
Your loving arms. I wish our
Days and nights were spent
together. I love you baby,
that is all.

A STAR LIGHT

Follow your inner light and let it shine so
bright. When you have been frighten by
the world, people, places and things
don't fear, you can change your path by
not fearing life. Always follow your inner
light and let it shine so Bright!
Remember you are a star in life, Fight!
Fight! Get yourself together and stay
right in life Live! Live, Long and strong
to the end of your Starlight.

THE PRIVATE TALK

David and I was sitting on the
Porch and we were listening to
his Momma and Daddy talking
at his house.
They were talking about David's
Big brother, the one had
David concern about The Private.
David started wanting to Know,
what was under the girls at church
Can, Can Dresses. David Momma
told his Daddy, David big brother
Percy, she caught five times with
different girls. She said, he was on
top of the girls in his bed in
their house. David, Daddy said,
that wiggling ass big boy needs
to get out and go to college!
He said, he was going to talk
with him before his Wee,
Wee, take sick and fall off.
I said, to David what's a
Wee, Wee?" he said, big
Brother Percy said it
something, that Big girls
like to have under their
Can, Can Dresses.
I said, David stop
talking about that,
cause my Momma said,
what's under Can, Can
Dresses is private.
Know little children
should talk about
their private,
especially
Little Kids like us.
David said, okay.

He said' De-ba
when I get older
I am going to
let you see
my Wee, Wee,
when you get
older and we come
from church you,
with a Can, Can
Dress on, will you
let me see where
my Wee, Wee
go De-ba.
I said, no! David
you not going see
my Bloomers!

BOBTAIL CAT

Tine let's stop to get Plums before
we continue to drive up the road
to Aunt Von house, let's get some
of those Sweet June Plums, from off
the side of the road.
Meow! Meow! Meow! Hell! What's that?
Tine! It's a Cat, a Black beautiful Cat.
Come Debra! Let's free the Cat, it done got
Its tail caught in the Plum tree. Hell nall!
that Cat might attack us.
Later that night I said, Tine, I should have
help you free that poor Cat.
The Rattlesnakes are probably going to eat
that Cat tonight.
Tine said Debra, go to sleep that Cat is miles
away and freed.

DISCO!

I was out there partying like
I was in a Broadway Show and
loved it.
I use to be partying in Mid-town
New York at, Bentley's, The Red
Parrot, The Ritz, the Paradise Garage,
The Down Under, The Underground
and Uptown Baby! The Bronx Disco's,
Jungle Fever, the Executive Playhouse.
I can go on and on naming some of
The Boogie Down Disco's, Hilltop,
Players Choice, Act- I & II, E&B, E&J
The Boca-Room and on.
The back in the day New York Disco's!
They was no club thing, like drinking
too much or eating too much. It was
all about people hooking up and Disco
Partying. We only needed a good D.J
to, put them 45's and Albums on.
It was no disking anyone back then
but everyone was doing a lot of kissing.
We were about, getting up on the dance
Floors and Partying like, we were Hot
Butter slipping off popcorn.
We were so happy to be somewhere!
Cool! Yes we were cool!
Partying laughing and having big time
fun together. Down at Disco's, DJ's
would be saying throw your hands,
in the air! Party like you just don't
care, to the beats, babies, bubbles,
now say," Oh yeah!" We said "OH Yeah!"
Damn! that was so, much fun. We did
just what the Bouncers wanted us to
and the DJ's wanted. We were good
to each other and the word,
R-E-S-P-E-C-T!

was not just a word it was an honor and
pleasure. People was not over drinking,
they were over Dancing. Some of them
including me would take off our shoes,
we were getting our Disco scuffle on.
I personally couldn't dance like I
needed to with no High Kneels shoes
on my feet. I had to wear them -calling
myself "looking-good! " Sometime now,
I be listening to the Radio Station
here in New York and they start
playing some of those Old
Jams, I say Oh Shit! I haven't heard this
in a long time. I get to dancing, more and
more off my disco cuts and anthems.
Come on now, I be in here forgetting and
missing appointments. I some time be late
for work, I be singing, I found love, I'll Take
you there, Get up do your thang, I know
you can do!
Billy Jean not my lover, show and tell me
that's the game people play when they
want to say, I love you. When I hear tear
the roof off and you don't stop rocking to
bang, bang boogies to Bee. I be singing,
dancing and laughing about the Good
old days at the Disco! Although we
paid a Small price to enter Disco's, back
in the day, I can tell you the experience
was priceless for me and so many others.
The Disco Parties brought out the best
things the Spirit and it was free. I am so
proud I can love the music bust moves
and transcend it feels good.
What you know about that?

DADDY WORD CREEPY

Daddy use to get on
my nerves with some
of the things he would
say. Daddy was very
smart but he acted
crazy a lot, mainly
when he was
smoking cigarettes
and drinking beer
at Aunt El Shop.
Daddy told my
Stepdad, If he ever
hear about him,
thinking or whipping
me for any reason,
if he did, he were
gonna make him kiss
his Jack Ass, Ass, out
in his Pasture.
My step Daddy said,
I don't whip children
Daddy said, that's a
good thing.
Daddy taught College
and were in world
War II, he were not
kidding.
I ask Daddy to stop
acting crazy one time
he laid in his yard on
the ground for about
three minutes quietly.
I said, Daddy what are
you doing? Daddy said,
you want me to die.
I said, no Daddy then
He jumped up off the

ground dust his suit
off and said, I got to
stay crazy to live
He said, Debit. I have
been places and seen
many things little one,
some men have never
been, never seen
and others were driven
to their death, I remain.
I said, Okay Daddy.
A man Daddy didn't
know well was at
Aunt El's Shop, he were
trying to pick up all the
local women, he kept
pulling out his Wallet
showing off his Money.
Daddy said, Green
Lizards show their
Money bag without
Sticking out their
Red tongues.
He told Aunt El sees
that man leaving like
that with ,Old Nellie
Pearl, he's a creep!
Daddy would never use
profanity but he would
analyze you and if he
did not like what he
learn about your
person in a nut shell
(minutes) as he use to
say, he would labeled a
person a Creep.
That was Daddy favorite
word for name calling, it
were either you were a

Creep or what you doing
was doing were Creepy.
Daddy wasn't Kidding
with you when he told
you those two words.
My father way with
words I inherited,
it's Creepy.

DON'T MISS OUT ON YOUR LIFE

People come and go throughout
One's life. We meet special people.
We love them, Family, friends, lovers.
Sometime we don't branch out from
our circle of people we know. We
can find pleasure in meeting and
knowing people in different places.
Those who are new and exciting
can influence our lives with something
new. We wake up and find years has
passed us by. We are not married,
have no children, never left the State,
Town, we were born in and never left
the Country. We feel stuck in town
with a job living one Paycheck from
being homeless. Take your profession
with you keep your mind open to learn
more. Stay safe don't let Life slip away
from you, it's a Great Big World to
explore out there, explore it as much
as you can. If you don't want to explore
the world alone, ask someone to be
your travel companion. If no one can
explore with you, hold God hands.
you will be guided to many people
travelling and viewing the World.
Anytime you get lonely, remember
to do phone home, there's a Road
to lead you back Home!

DEATH AND LIFE

Death is a Gift
from God Just
like Life.
Please let us all
stop doing things
to rush away our
Lives, our Brothers
and Sisters lives.
Let's stop causing
Death to our
people and get
back to respecting,
enjoying,
God's gifts.
mainly Life
and Living.

DEALING TO FEED OUR FAMILY

We who are gazing out the window
in the early morn not wanting to see
what we see but it's unavoidable to
the eyes, drugs and prostitution sales
continue to go on.
Nothing has changed same Dealers
same Whores.
Their stories haven't changed, they
say it's our jobs we need to survive
feed our families maybe one day we
will move out the hood and have a
better Life too! We want a house in
a nice little township, better school
for our Children and a job to change
our lives from what we do on the
Streets, if we live that long out here
in our positions. Remember us,
they say because we'll be driving
down these roads until we succeed.
Everyone else is right and we are
wrong.

DESEVRING A COMPLIMENT

I sat waiting to board my flight
to Atlanta Georgia I felt like
being playful. In the waiting area
an elderly lady sat next to me,
very beautiful in her mid-sixty
or early seventy she was well
dressed. I turn to her and said
you are a beautiful woman and
your outfit is becoming of you.
She said why thank you.
I replied why thank you.
She said that is a kind thing to
say. I said why you didn't
say it, she said what? I said
What? I told you, she said
What did you tell me? I said
you were a beautiful woman
She said what is your problem?
I said to her what's your problem?
She ask why are you talking to me
this way? I ask her why you are
talking to me this way? she said
get away from me Lady are you
funny or something-. I said no
are you funny or something. She
said you are full games, I said you
are full games. She said you started
talking to me first and I said you
started talking to me first. She said
what do you want? I said what
do you think? I want; she said ,
I really don't Know. I said ,
Ms. you were supposed to
compliment me back
by saying, I was beautiful too!
She start to Laugh and said, if
it's safe to say, outside of your

funny, entertaining and
craziness, young lady, you are
strikingly beautiful. I said
why thank you?

DO IT THAT'S ALL

She walks on the
Line stood behind
me at, The New York
City prestige's college
it's my freshman
year in college.
She said, loudly
behind me in line,
"I am going to be okay!"
Finally, I'm an Upper
Senior!
I am on line sweating,
after coming from my
fulltime Job. I am waiting
to get a part-time schedule
of Classes, the school
Cafeteria was hot, very
hot! I turn around, looking
her in her eyes. I wanted
to say, please shut-up! She
looked so friendly and
happy sharing her joy,
who was I? to rain on her
parade. She looked to be
older then I, both of us
were older than a lot of
the other students.
She ask me my name
school status, I told her,
I was a Part time Upper
Freshmen, she said,
soon you will be an Upper
Sophomore. She ask, how
was I doing in Class.?
I told her, okay but it is
hard work.
She looks at me and said,

wrong! I said excuse me
why did you, say wrong!
Like that!
She said, change your
attitude, today you
change, it right here and
now! She said," if you
are in college and think it's
easy, you need to get off
this line. If it was easy
everyone would be doing it!
So, you stay here get your
Assignments done and pass
Classes. I said," it's hard."
She gave me a look, I have
never forgotten. She were
staring confidence in my
eyes with her confidence.
She said, I am here to
Graduate and you are here
to graduate. She said, if I see
you walk these Halls, I don't
want to hear a complaint
from you. She said, you do
your Class work and
that's all, "you will graduate
doing your class work
that's all. I said, Okay I will
do it that's all.
She smile and said, they are
calling your name to register,
now. Do it that's all!

BILLY JOE!

You know me,
I know you.
Billy Joe!
Come on out
and let's do
What we do,
Bill Joe!
You know me.
I know you.
Billy,
Billy Joe!

HANKS

In the woods live some other kinds of humans far different from us. Momma say people don't believe in things they don't have much Knowledge about, they like to keep life simple mainly down here In the Woods of Alabama. Granddaddy and Momma never like to leave us ignorant about what has been reveal as living truth and proof of something. They say it's some other kind of people living in them Woods, they are not any Big Foots, no Mountain Men, no Indians, no strangers like any other of us humans. Granddaddy says you will only catch them out at night and they are not friendly to human like us and they can take any animal out in those Woods in a minute. He said, He been keeping eye on some of them for year he have seen what they have done to humans, animals and some of their capabilities, aren't nothing in the world like he ever seen or heard of. Grand-daddy went down his secret path to see them one day, their bodies were strange he said their nothing you could bare to look at, their verbal communication were off the chart unlike no sound one could imagine. Grand-daddy took four of us with him we were teenagers; he made us promise to never go back out there without him and never approach them HANKS. He said, He calls them Hanks because of how they live. He said, he never want us to touch them because they can live inside our bodies. Momma didn't want us to know about them she had touch one before my daddy were born and she had to live with a secret since. She said, she would not reveal her secret and said we should not be concern about seeking them Hanks. We saw something in them woods they had us afraid of the Woods and amazed. Grand-Daddy said, don't ever speak of the Hanks they showing up around the house at night. Granddaddy said, he will never tell the law because they will only come for them put them in cages to study them. They live there for years they only bothered, so far those who bother them. Grand-daddy says they not going to bothers any of us but they are never to be trusted because their dangerous and are an unknown kind. He said yawl stay away from those Hanks, just stays away from them. We said, yes Sir Granddaddy, we not going in the Woods looking for them Hanks.

DO KNOW MORE HARM TO BABIES

Exploiting the children
There are lots of us
can barely make the
bills. We don't go
around using our kids
as a meal tickets.
Allowing them to
Live their lives doing
Adult things selling
them and forcing them
to do Adult things,
allowing them to be
in harm way or killed.
You need to stop
harming our children.
If you don't want to
be parents don't have
children, their not for
you to abuse, use,
neglect or reject.
They're not little
people you give birth
to and give back. They
are God gifts to life.
You are not suppose
to quit on them,
their birth gives
you a life time Jobs.
What's wrong?
with you all anyway?
Do you get tired?
when they're not
listening, they
also get tired
when you not
listening.
Guess what?

You were like
that too!
So what if your
Parent didn't
Do this or that.
Your parent didn't
Decide to have
Your Babies, Now
so what.
Stand in your
Power! Do a better
job in the world.
Yes! Do better
for your children
than your
Parents did in
your life.
Use Knowledge
From family, books,
Websites sources.
Professionals and
other people
willing to help
you become better
people, Mommies
and Daddies.
You adults are
causing harm to
our Babies. What
you have
Psychological,
substance abuse
illness and issues.
Millions of people
have treated and
untreated mental
and substance
abuse illness. If
you are untreated

you need to get up
and go get help!
Get up, go get
it now!
Tell God,
Professionals-
Doctors,
Psychologists,
Social workers,
Churches,
Counselors,
Family, friends
Tell your problems,
ask for help and
guidance. You
need help
you're in trouble
no one can help
you if you don't
share the problems.
You will lose your
will and abilities if
you never seek help.
There is no shame
in asking for help.
If you don't get help
right away keep
asking and Praying
about it. Please keep
seeing as clear as
you can your
wrong doing
and stop !
You seek Help!
Professional
quality help from
the best possible
Providers.
Don't think about

having children
knowing you are
not ready, dealing
with Substance
Abuse and mental
 illness and only
have desire to
fulfill your
needs. You are
worth everything
when you need to
handle your,
business raising
your babies.
Your Mom and
Dad drama
don't have
anything to do
with your Babies.
Curb you finger
Straight.
Hell! A man or
woman has
a choice to
leave an unhappy
relationship but
before you get ill,
get to going. Make
sure you have a
supporting, time
to love, secure and
care for our babies.
Stop pointing your
Fingers at others
and calling out to
Old Blame!
Allow grandparent
to love their grand's.
You all stop lying

down making
Babies and passing
them off on your
parents and
grandparents, to
raise for no good
reasons. Who do
you think
you are living like
that? It's sad your
hands are free to
continue the same
cycle some of your
parents have led.
I see shameless
fools standing by,
hurting babies,
choosing
not to understand.
This is self-infliction
you causing to your
own flesh and
blood.
The world is
watching how you
doing the babies
wrong, so are the
babies.
It's not okay!
many of your
babies will
become adults.
They will surely
repay you for
causing their
suffering.
When you look
in the mirror
you see your

self, the pain
and suffering
cast on you,
Demonic.
Remember
God in you
and God is
forgiving.
Love our babies.
Let the babies
grow happy and
healthy they are
gift giving to you
to share with the
world.

CRACKED UP

All night long you hear her running. She's five feet
tall a mother, wife and my neighbor. In a day her
door slam about 15 times it's her or her company
she keeps. She has lost her way, she's turn from a
beautiful young, fun loving young woman to spooky.
She behaves in the most degrading manner, she lost
respect for herself, family and her world family.
She's cracked up. I ask God to enlighten her spirit
and bring her back to us. Times are so hard, I don't
think my little sisters, brothers or anyone should
intently use any drugs that takes away a clear
meeting of their mind. She is very scary to look at.
God in the Days of great Economic Depressions
please let us not crack up. She resemblance
pictures of all of us. If we don't show respect for
ourselves, we can become spooky, scary, and
kooky. We can't live our lives cracked up. I don't
wish that for any of my immediate Family or
World Families we need your contribution to our
World. I love you.

CHERISH LIFE

Life is so fragile
Just a fall to the
Ground can end
Physical life.
Cherish your life
and others lives
it's all we have to
share with each
other. Get back
close and in good
standard with
your love ones
we all strayed
away.
Now is the time
to go home and
make amends
and peace in your
life with those
willing to
open their Arms
to you. Don't
be afraid, listen
to the voice in your
head that hold your
safety, go on back
someone is missing
you.
The storms of life
are painful, cold and
bitter don't suffer
for no reason.
When you knock
Let go of the entire
created thoughts,
things and Just go
through the doors

bring God spirit and
love inside your
heart in the house.
You will be welcome.
Your enlighten spirit
helped you choose
one special door.
Now go on, someone
Love you and is
waiting.
If for any reasons you
Can't get to the door
make a call or send
letter. I love you and
wish you well.

DON"T DRESS ME

That man keep trying
to dress me up like
some Whore. He tells
me to wear short
dresses, show my Hips,
open the buttons to my
tops, show cleavage and
allow my Breasts to hang
out a little bit. I told that
man" I will not dress up in
outfits for him looking like
his Whore." He said its
sexy girl, many fine
women dress like that
and they wear their
Outfits with confidence!
I told that man, I am not
those women, what
they do is, just fine for
them and have nothing
to do with me.
He said "come on baby,
put on this fitted Black
Mini Dress with no bra or
bloomers! Put on them
high kneel shoes."
I am going to take you out
Tonight Downtown, New
York. I said, okay,
I will do what you want
under, these conditions.
He said, okay baby! I went
to the closet pulled out
tight fitted Black pants, I
bought, they were skin
tight, a Purple Ruffle
button down shirt

it was skin tight, Black
Leather Jacket skin tight,
Black Hat with a Purple
Ribbon and Bow on the
side of the hat and
sharp Black Leather
Ankle Boots. I said, here
man put this on, he said,
" What?" I said, put this
on Baby! I'm ready, so
you hurry, let's go!
He said, you're kidding right!
I said, hell no! We're going out
tonight. I'm dressed the way
you like and you dressed
the way I like. He put on the
clothes. He looks like a Gigolo-
man Whore and Hemp the Pimp.
We went out looking like that,
all that night. We looked like a
bag of Tricks. He got a lot of
attention from ladies and men
that night they thought he
were a star and they loved me.
When we return home he said,
woman, I had a good time and
many Laughs, partying
Downtown, in this crazy outfit
with you baby.
He said, you look sexy all
night. I said, Thank you baby!
I had fun too. He said, baby
I be damn if I will ask you to
wear something you don't want
to wear again. He said those
tight clothing was hurting me.
He said, "come with me to the
backyard. "I did, he took off his
Outfit, and burn all except the

Boots in a barrel, one by one.
He sang burn baby, burn these
Rags until they are all burnt out!
burning baby, please don't let
anything put it out! We laughed
so hard until Tears were falling
from our eyes. I told him, I'm
saving my outfit to get sexy for
him.

DOUBTS ON LIFE

You are not at the bottom
of pits! So, don't be sitting
around being useless, grasp
on to the positive life. You
are not useless. Let your
Person out of the box of
fairytales.
God will take you global.
You will find your purpose.
You are Alive! Live!
Life is priceless, celebrate it.
Your life is not define by
others and materialist things.
God work! You, have no
doubts on life and surviving.
You are alive! Live!

PISS! PISS!

Do you here them? Them loud mouth People, they're
not talking about nothing. Really! All they're talking
about is what somebody else did to somebody else.
What someone else said and how someone said it.
They talk loud about how people are not, what they
want them to be. Piss! Piss! Leave them people alone.
Do you hear? Them loud mouth People, they're not
talking about anything, they're just talking loud about
others Folks other than themselves, wasting breathe.
Them loud mouth people, is judging Folks, being haters
and bates. Do you here them loud Mouth people? You
know they're not talking about anything relevant to self.
Do you hear? Them loud mouth people, some of them
talks to much, loud and fast, they don't want to be
heard they just want to talk and be seen. Piss! Piss!
You here them loud mouth people Spoking words.
Piss! Piss! You just can't tune them out.

DON'T LET GO OF FAMILY TO DEATH

Some of our grandparents been gone
for a long time now, they left our
physical world. It seem like yesterday
they stood so proud providing moral
support and Love to the family. They
shaped how we love, Live and gather
for the Holidays and special occasions.
The deceased are truly missed in
Families. It doesn't matter their age.
The wonderful memories we shared
with them keep their and our Spirits
alive, they bring joy to our faces as
we remember. Our parent has started
to age they're not able to stand strong
as we remember, support them, and
care for them with Love as they age
and challenge the life changing process
of their bodies and minds. Let's remember
how they gave us moral support and love.
Remember the elderly understood your
Life values. Love your children, family and
Friends. Be a part of your families give
and receive love. Don't let go of the living
energy of our love ones Ancestors, who
has passed on to death their holding on
to us, to maintain Love of our Families.

EARTH LINKS

What is it you
seek to be,
living on this
Earth.
Do you know?
What do you
plan to do on
this Earth? Do
you know?
Whatever it
be make it
good deeds.
You will be
sharing it
with other
Earth
Links.
This Earth
is being
shared,
seriously!
One's power
On Earth
is no Larger
than
The brain
can think
and one
can carry
one's body.
Whatever
you going
to do, do it,
do it, very
well.
You know
what we

need from
you give it
to us, Earth
Links.
You know,
you should
give good
work and
Love to us.
You don't
want to give
nothing
else,
you know
what we need.
The Ancestors
has gone look
and pay
attention to
what they
have left us,
Warriors!
Now!
It's our turn,
we're not
trying
to end up in
Hell living as
Earth links.
Let all
of us stay
awake!
Look in the
World Mirror,
see how
Beautiful
Earth Links
are.
This World

is not created
for a few
People, it
belongs to all
Living creature
and Nature.
Earth Links.

BEING CONNECTED

In my Brain all I can carry is the ability to use the knowledge
in mind. In my heart all I can carry is the love and feelings I
have. With my eyes I can witness what I can see and as I see it.
With my ears I can hear sounds lifting the energy of my soul.
My skin crawl with feeling of sensuous beauty from my head
to my feet. Through nature the earth calls for my
understanding my relationship. I grow with the waters, wind,
sun, trees, flowers, other animals and creations of God.
Not taking the opportunities to explore the wonders of our
world I have lost truth of some of my human identity.
I need to migrate explore the world with my gifts given.
I need freedom, being, confine to one country does not
define my person. The world is too large to stay in limited
places. I need to keep new knowledge circulating in mind.
My heart needs to share love in the World and feel love.
My eyes need to be open to experience the natural and
created world. I need to observe different visionary sites.
My ears need to know other sounds to lift my soul and
energy. I need to travel the earth lands, feel the sensation
of goose bumps touching my skin while experiencing
the new. Through the nature of things earth energy calls
upon us we are, where we belong, it shows us what we
need to understand. There are no good reasons we
should live life with a sense of enslave captivity. We
must acknowledge our freedom comes when we
connect to our earth links and universal surroundings.

BEAT UP IN LOVE

All beat up!
I can't take it anymore
I am so beat up, my
mind just won't leave
my heart alone about this.
I am on painful love, I am
carrying it around like
a flaming torch that won't
burn out. There is nothing
happening, the one I love
don't love or want me,
I know this.
I am so damn fixated with
being in love with someone
that don't Love me, I was told
stay away. What in the hell
is the problem. Why can't we
just love, love one another it
would easy my pain.
My beat up thoughts
came kicking out of my mind,
making my heart pound and
breaking me down. The facts
telling me, I am in love alone.
I am so beat up, this kind of
Love it is the loneliest love I
ever known.
I can't set it free, I have tried
but the feelings won't go
anywhere. Feeling! I want
you to just go away and die!
I simply have fell in love. I
have no one to share my
loving feeling with.

A TEXT MESSAGE TO MR. HARD

Hey! Mr. Hard
tell my Good friend Mr. Dick I
lost my hairy Black Pussycat.
She's in heat Mr. Hard she
will come for Dick. Dick loves
my Black Hairy Pussycat.
She's crazy for Dick too!
She's usually a good Girl, Dick
will find her and common her
hot behind down. Please get
Dick, Hard for me and bring
him straight to my door
beautiful Pussycat will come
running out of hiding for Dick.
Mr. Hard you have no idea
how this sweet, Black, hairy
and heated Pussy Cat love
and work Dick.

A CONFESSION

I love one man
seven days a
week. He don't
share my loving
feelings I know.
I don't want to
forget him, I
don't know if I
could if tried, it's
been going on
now for years
since we met
and parted. We
decided we
could not be in
two place at the
same time. It's
been hard and
painful loving
him like this.
He chose his
place and I
chose mine. I
thought my
feeling for him
would fade
away with time,
it been years and
the mere thought
of him send my
heart racing as if
he is going to
entered through
the door of my
home again, like
right now!
I can't shake it

off. I keep having a
recurring dreams
of him holding me
in his Arms with
my head on his
chest near his
heart, I could
hear it beat, beat
and beat. Just
before I awake
he whisper in
my Ear, baby I
love myself you
baby.
I awake with my
eyes wide open
checking the
other side of the
bed where he use
to lay when we
were together, I
see no him. He's
not there with me.
My heart's
ponding, for what
once were
and is no longer. I
took a deep
breathe and came
to conclude, I am
dreaming. I love
myself some him,
I confess, I always
will. I never had a
love so sweet and
kind like the one
I found with him.
I never got enough
of being with him,

loving him, kissing
him and being
intimate with him.

A JETTISON POEM

To jettison throw over board to lighten a craft, discard, throw away
or drop something. In life the meaning of jettison need to be applied,
when we take on others problems and sometime end up carrying
extra heart breaks and disappointments. We need to stay dear to
God, ourselves, Love ones, friends and to passing strangers sometime.
It's okay, give out the good in your heart to all that allow you to.
You should never bring in your company people or things you do
not wish to be a part of. People can bring you a load of unnecessary
trash. You may have to do a jettison! to get rid of them, you don't
have to carry around their extra weight. You can be kind to them
but let them know not to get to close, to fast to your person or peace.
Right now! Jettison your unwanted baggage you'll stay light on your
feet. When you see someone coming with a load of junk even words
from their mouths, with no meaning to you or anything to do with
who you are, be good to them and remember Jettison meaning
above. Grab your person, your good heart and run, jump, leap, take
flight from them, their problems, they're not yours so don't allow
them to weigh you down with their unwanted baggage.
RUN!

AIN'T COMING IN MY HOUSE

I don't need them men
and women crowding
round my door they
ain't know friends of
mine. I say! what they
wanna come up in
here for. I ain't got
nothing for them. They
ain't going to get all
Laxie-daisy up in my
House. See! I ain't got
nothing for them.
I ain't given them any
of my some things to
eat, and my Whiskey is
for my folks only. I be
damn if I got any that
dope some them be
tripping on, up out
there! So if by chance
yawl in my neck of the
woods and you think
you wanna pay
someone a visit, hear
me loud and clear
yawl best skip leaning
 and knocking on my
door. Hell Nall,
Skippers! Ain't nothing
in here for you and you
can't come in!

FEAR OF REJECTION

She has a feeling for him,
the first day she saw him
he walked into a Medical
Office.
She never saw him before
when, he walked through
the door she looked up
from the book she was
reading. She scanned his
handsome body from
head to toe as, he
proceeded to walk pass.
He was dressed, in his
Suit and Shoes made
for the prince he appears
to be. As he passed her,
she couldn't reframe from
saying something to him.
She said, with no hesitate
in a crowded Midtown
New York Medical Office
Reception
area to him, "Wow!
you look good, he
looked at her with
a gleam in his eyes
and a charming
smile and said"
Thank you." He
continued to walk
to his Office.
He's a sexy Italian
man, fine dresser,
smart and a pleasure
to see. She soon had
the pleasure to meet
him later he became

her doctor. She can't
hold back feelings,
she has for him they
show on her face every
time she in his present.
She's not bold enough
to tell him about the
passions she feels for
him. She can't get
through a day without
having moments of
loving thoughts about
him. He turned her on,
the very first time she
saw him. She can
visualize being there
for him, as a friend,
loving him consoling
him and holding true
to him. She wants so
much to tell him of
these feelings.
She fears rejection.
She know, he knows
she like his sexy fine
ass and would love
to kick it or just get
busy with him. She
doesn't knows his
feelings about all the
stuff going on in her
head but sometime
he gives her a look
as if he might want
to visit her in bed.
If he gives any clarity
about wanting to get
to know her outside
of his work she

will be pleased. She
would go around the
world and back
with him to get the
opportunity to know
and be with him. She
gets nervous at the
thought of saying
something to him
about her feelings.
She remains
uncommitted to
anyone and hope
he does to until she
could get the nerves
to express her feelings
to him she says, stay
tune, she's going
to tell him her feelings.

ATTENTION

You need to stop!
Attention!
Look at you and me.
My love needs are
shouting out my
body.
I got moves and
mood.
Come see how
my body is prep
to work out.
I need to touch
you. I need your
touch.
Can we caress?
Come to me,
with your body
and mind.
This body of
mine needs
loving.
I am waiting
for your Push
Power to feel
my warmth,
my warmth
inside.
Attention!
My hair, eye
nose, Lips,
tongue, full
body is in
vibration.
I want to
share
my rotating,
pulsations,

and love
sensations
with you.
Attention!
My body got
moves and
my mind got
mood.
Thank you.
It's a pleasure
to unite our
bodies
spreading
love. Now we
are in bound
spiritually,
naturally,
in route to
transform
and transcend
into one.

AFTER ALL THESE YEARS

After all these years, I thought
I was done. Then just the other
day, I thought I saw you. Every
feeling I have for you just came
raising my heartbeat, after all
these years. Just the first sight
of you made me want to be in
your arms again. After all these
year, I thought I was done. I
can't get over you, seeing
your Being makes me want
to be in your company, be
imitate with you. I know
I should move on after this
long time being apart from
you. I still can't get it
together. Every time I see
you or think of you, I can't
help reaching out for you.
After all these years, I
thought I was done. If
only you knew how
much I still want to love
you. The thought of you
bring back our Journey of
sweet times together.
Baby the loving we shared
felt like it was brand new.
After all these years
I thought I was done.
It may have been years
of lust for you, you have
always been my
sexy love baby and my
love at first sight, I love
myself some you baby.
When I thought, I saw

you the other day,
Butterflies, took over, I
always told you, you give
me, they took over,
reaching every part of
my body. My loving
feelings I have for you
came with intense racing
heart beats, I will always
run to you.
After all these years, I
thought I was done.
There is no done place in
my heart I have Love for
you, sweet love. After all
these years, I thought I was
done. What is done when
you have someone,
in the world you to love?

BUG EYES WITH ME

I found my old
Bug Eyes.
While doing my
apartment
Spring cleaning,
I came upon
them, they
sat in a corner in
my closet in a
Black Case.
I was shocked,
I just knew they
were in that case,
I just knew it!
Just as they were
in my sight staring
at me waiting
for our reunion
I were Staring
too!
In the late 1980's
and Mid 1990's
Bug Eyes and
I were almost
inseparable.
I thought Bug
Eyes were
Lost in New
York City
Streets, at
the College
I attend or
maybe at my
old good City
Job. Years
had passed
between old

Bug Eyes and I.
I had gotten
older and so
had Bug Eyes
It's the year
20-10 everyone
Need a good
friend.
I thought of
the days
Shared with
Bug Eyes, Bug
Eyes saw
me through
a lot of hard
times tough
times helping
me while I
read, write
and erase
my way
through life.
I reach over
to pick up
the case
Bug Eyes
had been
resting so
comfortably
since our
years apart.
I shook it and
then I heard a
rambling noise
it was Bug Eyes
alright, waiting
to get, out I knew
I should take
a peek first

because Bug Eyes
would shine in
your Face when
you peek
in the case.
I open the
Case, Bug
Eyes saw
me peeking,
I said, WOW!
It's you!
The case flew
open it was
Bug Eyes
looking at
me with a
fuzzy dust
on. Bug Eyes
couldn't take
being dirty, I
hurried and got
Bug Eyes
cleaned up.
I said I miss
you Bug Eyes!
Bug Eyes
was shining
It seems as if
Bug Eyes
was saying
tries me on,
try me on,
What you
waiting for
go on you
Just try me on.
I put Bug Eyes
on my head
I could see the

room light up
and every
thing looked so
clear. It were
like Bug Eyes
had never left
or gotten lost.
Our joining back
together were
a sight for soar
Eyes.
BUG EYES
and I again
join together
to do great
things.
Bug Eyes
assured me
we would
not part until
I see my way
clearly through
to travel,
succeed on
a rewarding
and new
path.
No! I am not
letting Bug Eyes
out of my
sight. Bug Eyes
going to be
with me
shining
directly off
my face.

ASK FOR FORGIVENESS

He looked at her and said you remind me
of my past, when I were out there partying
to the break of dawn, running up, down
Streets of New York with all kinds of women,
drinking and drugging my life away. Yes, this
was my life style, spending up my money just
running, running out in the Street of New York
cheating on my wife, my so call girl friends,
gambling with the boys. I were living the life of
a single man and acting as if my wife were never
there, you were not even there. I were doing
what I wanted to and I really didn't give a damn.
He looks at her and said, I have changed now! I
accepted God in my life., I have put down
chasing women, drinking, Drugging and gambling.
Yes Lord! I have put down my past sins. He ask
her what bring you back home to live in Alabama?
She said to him I have had my sinful times, I never
want to Live that way and I take responsibility for
my sins. I apologize to all I have cause pain. She
said to him I never were a part of your sins, I was
a victim of them. Yes, I was a victim. If you have
changed and accepted God, God sent me home
because this is where I wanted to be for so long
this is the place I love my home. This is our
chance meeting Ex-spouse you are supposed
to apologize to me for the hurt you caused me,
the pain and suffering I went through, this is
why I stand before you. I have accepted life and I
follow instructions and share my enlighten
experiences. I am a woman of God.
I apologize to you for pain and suffering I
caused you. Please forgive me. Let God Know
your sorrow and ask for forgiveness too, ask me
for forgiveness. The next time you see me or
think of me you will never have to tell me, I
remind you of your past again.

God going let you know your past has gone.
I am only here for the present, ask for
forgiveness, forgiveness will set you free of
your past it won't matter why I am here you
will know while we live in the present.

BIG BOY

Lil Sister constantly
told all of us girls in
our Dorm
Sisterhood crew
about her brother
Big Boy.
She spoke highly
of him and how she
wanted one of the
older girls to meet
him. She talked
about how handsome
he were and how
much of a gentleman
he were. All the girls
wanted to meet him
because girls like nice
guys. During a spring
Holiday Break, Big Boy
came to visit his Lil
sister Pat on Campus.
All of us girls in the Dorm,
our crew, were happy to
know some new guy off
Campus would be visiting
around our Campus and
bringing other guys for us
girls to meet.
They attended another
University in a State two
hours away from our
University. They all were
Seniors, three of us were
Seniors and the other two
Juniors. They came to our
campus and met with us
they were fine, all of them,

we met them briefly and
was invited to hang out
with them for the weekend.
They had their hotel
Reservations and were
ready to party, we were
ready. We ate dinner at the
Hotel, boys treat. Then we
entered their Hotel Suite.
It was five girls and five
boys, Yep! the party was
on. The girls ranged from
5'3 to 5'6 feet, weighting
about 105 to 125 and the
boys 5'7 to 6'1 feet,
weighting about 160 to
200 they were stacked.
Yep! We all were 18 years
old and older. We had an
introduction Dance Party
a girl dance 1st and tell
their name and interest.
Then a boy dances 2nd and
tell his name and interest.
Everyone had took their
turns until all ten of us
was casually introduced.
the party was on! Music
setting it off, our dance
moves made it feel like
we were in a Dance
Theater, Booty shaking
Hands in the air and all
that good stuff Ohio
Players Skin Tight playing.
The boys shared a wonderful
Weekend with us girls we
loved Big Boy and his friends.
We all were paired off

and guest who got paired
with Big Boy? Yes!!!!!!!!!!
It was me yours truly and
let me tell you Big Boy was
just as kind and sweet as
his Lil sister described him,
that country boy rock
my boots for over five
years after college.
He got me still looking
for him. If anybody
knows the where about
of Big Boy tell him, his
Honey Sucker Rose, will
be please to meet with
him. He can call me,
Email me, text me,
he can XO, XO me from
the sky. Lil sister and
Lisa, I here you are still
with those two boys
from the hotel Parties.
Perry and Jim, those are
Big Boy's good friends
you all, Let Big Boy know
he got his Honey Sucker
Rose, she is still looking
for him, tell him the sight
of him will be enough,
Babies!

DAYS GOING TO THE DUMP YARD

Let's not forget where we came
From, let's not forget those days after
Momma left and we were even poorer
More than before.
My daddy didn't care much about
caring for us children, he really didn't
know how. We were cold, lonely
after Ma-dear left us to save her life
from My Daddy. Ma-dear later return
for us and saved our lives. Remember
what we choose to forget about
living in our birth states.
We had it very hard historically in
Alabama being Black being called
Niggers, being raped, beating,
killed and mistreated we got
no respect as people, not even
from Government controlling that
racism State, it were enough
dealing with our family problems.
Our foundations of Families life
were broken apart, after our
mother left. We had been left ,our
eldest sister took care of us in the
absence of our Mother and Father.
My eldest sister will always be my
hero, may she rest in peace.
God sent us an Angel to guide us.
Thank God for my eldest sister.
Some people these days have no idea
What It was like and what it is still
like to be poor. Poor Black and White
families were going to the Dump Yards.
The Dump Yards use to be our
Supermarket, shoe store,
Clothing store and any other
stores depending on what we found.

Our neighbors and we would make
three Trips a week to the Dump yard
and if we didn't We would go without
shoes, clothing, food and other
things that helped our basic needs.
We some time were chased by wild dogs
going and coming from the Dump Yard,
we had to fight them off with sticks and
big Rocks, wild dogs were not going to
stop us from surviving. The Dump Yard is
a place I never wanted to think of again
after mother came and got us from
Daddy House in Alabama and took us to
New Jersey. I never saw one again, until
we moved to New York it was a Dump
Yard on a hill on the road to Orchard
Beach, City Island in the Bronx, New York.
Alabama is my home. I love the beautiful
Countryside of Alabama State, I truly do.
Alabama need to change. People were
force to leave their homes to seek jobs in
other states. If I could change any State in
the United States it would be, the State
of Alabama. When people from foreign
countries leave Countries and come to the
United States don't you dare look down
on the people in our country. Many of
us have not been given an opportunity
to be the best we could be in our home
Towns, we still got people with Dump
Yard stories in our Countries and in the
world, this need to change for all of our
Towns. Let's change it for our babies now,
the ones to come, let's help teach others,
together we can do remarkable work and
turn our dreams into reality. Oh what a
little love for humanity won't do or can do.

MA-DEAR

Ma-Dear you are a strong proud woman.
You are beautiful, soft spoken, kind, warm.
You love your family, humanity, and you
Love the Earth.

Ma-Dear you were not afraid to walk the
Southern Roads, or go into the Woods
alone. I guess, that why Daddy called
you his **Real Country Girl.**

Ma-Dear seeing you in your Garden
Picking Collard Greens, Peas, Corn,
Tomatoes Okras and Peppers, I know
we are going to have some good
Supper.

I admire you Ma-Dear I am Happy to
have you as my Ma-Dear. The sun in
your sandy brown Hair, you're pretty
hazel, eyes reflexes the colorful,
Cotton Flare, Dress you wore.

Ma-Dear we are in Alabama in the early
60's you and My-Daddy is keeping the
family together. Yawl's show is the
Partying kind, so is Big Mama.

Big Mama Café. A lot folks in these
Alabama Counties show like being around
Yawl, they come miles to be down at the Café.

Yawl's at the House Partying every Friday.
On Saturdays yawl's down in Sweetwater
partying in Big Mama Café.

Good-o Sweetwater, Alabama, Big Mama's
Café, that Jukebox fill with many hit record

songs. Ma-Dear, I love Mama's Café, she got
them-two-for-a-penny-butter-cookies-coconut-
Bars too! Mama has all the Toms snack products
and more.

Ma-Dear I am enjoying some Potted Meat and
saltine crackers now. I show would like a Pepsi
or Royal Crown drink to wash my some-eat
down. Mama got one of them big cold water
Box with a heap of drinks.

Yes, Ma'am! I can Drank a whole one, Ma-Dear.
Listening to that Juke-Box all **Yawl's** keep calling
a **Rock-Ola.** I just Love to hear those 45 songs.

Ma-Dear, I don't want to be gone-up-to-know
Aunt El's House, ain't no Rock-Ola up yonder.
 Ma-Dear get me out of Granddaddy old car,
let me stay down here and dance Rock and Roll.

Ma-Dear! Ma-Dear! That's Blues man **Tommy
Tucker** record playing on the Rock-Ola! Is that
Yo-favorite song?

Turn me loose! Let me out this Old car,
Granddaddy! Let me dance and sing on this
Alabama land, to my Ma-Dear favorite Song.

Turn me loose! **Tommy Tucker, Song, Hi-Heel
-Sneakers!** Put-on- your- Red-Dress-Baby-cause
we-going-out-tonight. Put-on-you Hi-Heel-
Sneakers-just- in -case-some-fools-might
want-to-fight.

Ma-Dear I remember you saying, child, Please!
Git, your little fast self-back in Daddy's car with
the other children to go get ready for bed.
Granddaddy shook his head and said, Lord!
"Rie, **Lil- Deb-it** is some-thin else."

BUSY DEVIL

The devil is
busy.
If it is in your
company you
need to pull
up a seat, it's
going to be
hell surrounding
your life.
There'll be pits
of fire and Fork
poking at your
peace on Earth,
cause by you
inviting it in your
Life. There will be
God forces against
you. Make a choice
to lead the devil
away from your
company there is
no purpose for it
being your guest.

ABSORBING

You can't absorb everyone
misery, if you find yourself
doing such a thing, you will
lose much of your own
happiness. Pay attention to
your mental needs, for your
peace and happiness in your
lifetime.

ACHIEVERS AND WANNA B'S

The achievers jumps through
Hoops to get knowledge
needed for success. They
take paths to accomplish the
things they need. They don't
stop until they complete their
set goals. Then they go walking
down the roads to do something
new. They achieve by putting
in work, spending long hours
to get their jobs done. The
Achievers live to give back
something to the world and
then they reap the benefits.
The Wanna B'S, can be
Achievers but the Wanna
B'S are not going to put in
Know hard work. The
Wanna B'S hit the road and
start down what they call
easy street. Wanna B'S has
no plans to make millions,
their out to take millions.
Ponzi Scams, rob, kill, steal
and fall short of Academic
Achievements. They live
above their means.
They never complete a,
successful goals. Wanna B'S,
want something for nothing.
They really not interest in
working to give back to
anyone, only themselves.
Achievers never want to be,
Wanna B'S it's not in their
Nature. Wanna B'S don't
want to know how to an be

Achievers, they are
Wanna B'S it's not in their
Nature. The Achievers are
like Reality, Wanna B'S are
like Fantasy they walk
different paths. It's not
good for them to meet
up or hook up they weigh
each other down. There is
no common good in them
partnering.

A THOUGHT OF YOU

I tried to challenge the thoughts, of you. I
wished thoughts away as, they came in my
mind. I thought, asking myself, why I have
urges to reminisce about you and me ?
Then one thought came, one, after another.
I sat alone thinking of our sweet moments
shared, intimate, caressing, passionate
love we making, your kisses. It's taking my
breathe away, our gift giving to one another,
soft whispers, of us sharing a forever love.
Thoughts of hand holding, laughter, our walks,
shopping, family time, friends and the fun we
enjoyed. I am still flattered by the thought of
how every meal, I cooked were your favorite,
it gave me happiness to know you enjoyed
my recipes. Then I thought, we are now so far
apart, I Trimble, it's senseless for me, having
thoughts of us once being together. I said, I'm
not thinking this! Then I thought I must accept
to my Mind and Heart it matters. The thoughts
were of remembrance, of you, I, time and place
in our lives being together were, Joyful and
pleasing. The feelings, being with you made me
feel like, I could reach a Star as, long, as I knew
we would be there holding hands smiling,
shining, like that star together from
the far distant.

COMING OF AGE YAWL

Mid fifty,
we should see life in
a different light.
As we aged Family,
Friends, others. We
pass on, the young
are getting sick and
passing on in an
alarming numbers.
The inter Circle
of family and friends
you can see what lost
we share when
those someone's we
love is no longer
able to be there for
us, it's painful but yet
we have our memories.
Stop! Remember,
a funny time shared,
a time walking pass a
Rose garden on a Spring
day, sitting
on the porch or standing
on the street with love
ones, talking about things.
Crying to them about the
present, talking about the
future, wedding day,
informing them of your
first born and child bearing
years. Think of all life
celebrations you shared
with them. When the world
treated you cold and no one
else could understand your
pain. You knew that one of

those in your inner circle
would listen, talk it out with
you or walk it out with you.
They were there to help you,
improve your life not help
you destroy yourself or others.
Those of us who has became
Adults and Younger can see
the faces of love one elderly,
young, family and friends and
World families are becoming ill
and fragile, passing on. When we
see people struggling we need
to help them live out their live
peaceful. No children or
institution should rob them of
that. We will live become Ill,
elderly, sick and fragile. We
need to Kneel before God
every Day and ask for our well
care and our people, know
Heaven has accepted those,
who has given their last
breathed? They are back with
energy the creator.
Reflect on all that you
know. Help those of us
in the Physical World
walk, talk and care for
those whom has lost
their way or is suffering?
In times of illness,
transitioning sit with
by them hold their hands
and pray. The nature of
things, Will allow all of us
to make a transformation,
its life. Volunteer.

BESTY PEARL

Granddaddy were
telling Mama that
Old! Betsy Pearl
done clearly, gone
and lost her mind.
Mama said, what
you talking about
Papa? Granddaddy
Said, Betsy Pearl can't
sleep at night since
David Lee built that
great big beautiful
home across the
road from her. She
done plum lost her
cottoning picking
mind. David Lee is a
hard working man
and his Daddy was
always proud of him
and his success.
That boy always
helped and loved
his folks. He
graduate Marengo
High in his youngling
years. Betsy Pearl
always wanted to
married him but
Betsy Pearl would
have pulled him
down. The only one
Betsy could take
home was Ike and
have babies, so
Ike gave her what she
wanted. He kept her

bare feet and Pregnant
the life she wanted.
Now she got nice
Thangs but I think she
don't want David Lee
to enjoy his nice
Little Wife and thangs.
Mama said, Papa how
David Lee feels about
Betsy Pearl, he haven't
saw her in a long time.
Granddaddy said, he
sees her as a long lost
friend.
David Lee and his wife
talk with her at church
and wave from their
car at her when passing
her house.
David Lee said, since
she Live on the opposite
side of the road from him
She always standing
on the porch waving.
when he leave home.
He heard her telling
Family and mutual
Friends about
everyone visiting
his home. He said
Betsy Pearl wants
to know what kind
Refrigerator they
have, Livingroom
furniture, Bedroom
furniture, Draws the
they wear and
anything,
mostly about him.

He said Betsy Pearl
Even come to help
his wife Susan plant
yard Flowers it seems
as if she's trying
anything to get close to
me he said. David Lee
said, he had to put his
foot down with Betsy
Pearl, he said Betsy
Pearl were telling
some of the Town
people him and her
was coating again,
he said, he ask her
about it she said,
she never said
anything like that
so he said he
believe her. Until
one day his wife said,
Betsy Pearl told her,
he wanted her like he
wanted Sweet Potato
Pie.
She told his wife
Susan, he said, that's
why he move back
here in Dixon Mills,
Alabama. He wasn't
here, just to retire
but he came to
be her love again.
He said, she told
Susan, I never did
Like you coming to
my home with my
old man, with your
bony Lil Self, don't

you know you have
never equal to me
in David Lee mind
and heart. David Lee
said his Wife Susan
said, Betsy Pearl was
looking crazy, like a
wild eye Rat coon,
she were shock and
fearful of her life.
David Lee were not
Home so she told her
to leave and Betsy
Pearl stood with her
hand on her Hips
looking her up and
down and said, what if
I don't you man stealer.
Little Detroit, Michigan,
City Hoe, Susan trying to
steal my Man David Lee!
Susan said to, Betsy Pearl
What is wrong? Then
Betsy Pearl left out her,
House leaving the door
wide-open.
She started Screaming as
she were crossing the
Road to her house,
BESTSY PEARL!
Betsy Pearl!
is what! You said what?
What's wrong! Wrong
with Betsy
Pearl! Betsy Pearl! Then
she went in her House.
When David Lee got
Home he found his poor
Wife upset from the

incident.
Susan told him what
happen. He went over
to Betsy Pearl House
and knock on the Door
Betsy Pearl came to
the door butt naked,
David Lee said he
were shocked.
He said, Betsy Pearl
stood as if she were
disconnected from the
world.
She told him
I am so glad you
Came, come in, I got
you some Supper
waiting. Granddaddy
said David Lee Knew
something were wrong.
He jump off the porch into
the Yard and were standing
on Betsy Pearl front lawn.
When he saw granddaddy
drive by he waved for him
to come to the house.
Granddaddy came and stop.
Granddaddy knew both of
them all their lives, from the
yard. Granddaddy told Betsy
Pearl to get dress and let him
come in the house to use her
telephone and she did.
Granddaddy called her
brother and sister to come
see about her, while they
waited for them in
Betsy Pearl, yard.
When Betsy Pearl folks

got there she took off
running at 65 years old
she couldn't out run her
younger brother and
sister she got caught.
Granddaddy said. Betsy
Pearl sister said, she had
stop taking her medicine
for a whole week and lost
her mind. Granddaddy
said, David Lee said, it
made him sad to see her
like that and there is a lot
of folks like Betsy Pearl
needing someone to
be with them 24 hours in
a day. Mama said, Papa
that is right guess that
why Betsy Pearl nieces
move in with her from
Selma, to help her. The
Lord will Bless them.
Granddaddy nod his
head and said, show will
Gal, show will.
Chat Note: Mental Illness
Awareness

FOUR-THE –TOE

Hey! What's up?
FOUR-THE-TOE.
It's me Bliff, Bliff!
I am back on the
Block, come over
to my Mom's House.
It's gone be Bliff,Bliff
and FOUR-THE-TOE
going out tonight.
We can go rolling
Downtown to Party
with some cuties.
FOUR-THE-TOE said,
"Hey, Bliff, Bliff!
FOUR-THE-TOE
is handling Dollar
Bills, Don't go
shaking your
Pockets for
nothing, Man!
Bliff, Bliff said,
that's my Man,
the one and only,
FOUR-THE-TOE!

CHANGING IN THE NAME OF GOD

We need to change, we have committed
sins in the sight of God. God has grant us
the good we needs to see our wrongs
and make them right. We have turned
our faces away from our Religious
upbringing, adopt by us since birth
from our ancestor and parents. We have
laid Bibles down far too long and doing as
we please, seeing only fit what we have
chosen to do. We bypass the churches and
 head for the clubs. We give up our Tithes
money for gambling and trying to hit a
lottery. We loved married men and
married women as if it is no problem. We
put alcohols, drugs and Tobacco in our bodies
and other foreign substance. We have told
lies we were not proud of. We have laid our
bodies next to men and women we did not
love or know for money to care for our families,
to care for us and to care for our children. While
we sin we have never stop sitting with God
present and nor have we ever have been
disbelievers. We have never challenge God's
work because we are always Enlighten and
cannot. We have been experiencing our
connected Energy with God since conception
early before birth. In Childhood signs of God
present surrounds us, it is something you
cannot ignore. Many of us have stayed away
much too long from the temples and houses
where God people are doing work, building
strong people, moral and communities in
societies. This day forward we need to change
and look within to see and understand the
God in us, stay away from the Sins causing us
suffrages. We need to change, enter temples
and houses where God's people are in

communities doing his work, healing.
God expect us to make our changes and
God messages is to be delivered to all his
people, God will accept you and lead you on
the road of righteousness, let you discover
deep within your true purpose and being
on earth, as in heaven. Stop Fighting the
Highest Energy let go and experience the
Natural of things. Our seeds are made to
bloom natural and free.

I LOVE MY CHILD

I am a mother, I love
my child. I wish all
good things for my
child. I love to see
the growth of my child.
I watched my child
growth and I watched
as my child enter
adult years. I am
proud of my child.
I watch other people
Children and I am
proud of them too.
When you have seen
a Child grow from a
Infant in to an adult.
It's a beautiful
experience seeing
little people that use
to need you so much
doing positive adult
things in the world.
It's good to see they're
all grown up. I love my
child, God bless my
Child, God Bless your
Child.

MAN JUMPING AISLES

I were shopping in the
Supermarket a cold
Winter Evening, notice
this man about my age
wearing a dark brown
mink three Quarter's
Coat, he was Jumping
around from aisle to
aisle every aisle I come
out he would go in.
He were just smiling
That cold winter
evening.
Finally he came
In the aisle where I
were with his crazy
acting self. He bump
into me and said
excuse me Little
shorty, I look at
him he were a
handsome tall Guy
calling me shorty
I said, you think you
Cute, don't you be
jumping around
In the store aisles.
He patted me on my
butt and said, yes
Shorty just like that
little Bump I patted.
Now may I have a
number?
I said no! Your
evaluator doesn't
go to the top, I
think you Crazy.

He said okay but I
think You're cute.
I said "Thank you
But no more butts
touching to night,
he said okay shorty.
We laugh and he
Took his cute crazy
self-down another
aisle, I went to the
Checkout line.

SHE WALKED THE RED DIRT ROAD

She walked alone down the country
Red Dirt Road carrying just herself
and her belongings to catch the school
bus for a year in the winter wearing
her Hat, Pea Coat, Gloves
Britches and Ankle Boots. She carried
a shoulder Pocket book. She walked a
half a Miles from home down that
country Red Dirt Road and a half
mile back every day.
She carried herself well. On both
side of the road covered
with brown dry Grass and
Pine Trees. She goes walking that
Red Dirt Road.
Those early mornings come rain or
Sunshine she would walk the road.
She struts down that Red Dirt road,
never looking back. She moves with
confidence and grace. She looks
forward to completing her education
and goals as, she travel that Red Dirt
Road. She is preparing for her future
and for a journey to lead her from
walking down that Red Dirt Road.

A FAVOR

I ask someone for help. I had to ask
myself, what would their help matter?
Why do I need their help? What
Different will their help mean to me?
After receiving help most importantly,
I have to thank them very much. After
taken, receiving, what I asked to be
given, I have to find a gift of equal
wealth to return to the one helping me.
I also must help some else needing my
help. I believe that there is life cycle
we have no control over, It's a Cosmic
force from our energy. The more
aware the better we understand it.
Oh! We will return a favor.

HATERED OF THE SELF

I don't care who you are or where you
came from. I don't care what color you
call yourself. You are Human!
I don't care what your beliefs are.
You are human! When you have
awaken in a God given day, you should
be happy and enlighten with another
chance of being a human being on Earth,
the only planet in the universe we
know people like us exist. If you rise in a
day with hatred in your, heart and in
your Mind, know it's no secret. You
have to face yourself. Your hatred is not
reflexing all the wonderful people of our
Earth, your hatred is a deep rooted
hatred called you. You are human!
Look at you can you see you.

GRANDDADDY AT THE SHOP

Granddaddy said" every time Mr. Les-Earl
Come out his house he be sharp as a
Whistle.
Granddaddy said there are some thangs
I show don't like bout that rascal, one
is he wear that loud smelling Bugs spray
men perfume, Granddaddy
said" and two his britches be too tight.
Granddaddy said Three that rascal ain't
born with no manners dot-damn-mit!
The forth thang Granddaddy said
was that boy always run up
in the toilet at my house smelling it up
with his old! Doddle boot-a, it seems
like every time he's here he runs
his doddle boot-a up in the toilet
in my House, when I got to go up in
there". Granddaddy says to
Grandmamma "Gal that boy is a
fool! He still don't know not to eat
that food his Lil wife Cattail feed him
before heading out the house to
come down here to the Shop,
where all these here Pretty women
come to swing Dance on Friday nights.
Go tell that boy, Gal that Cattail is
Putting some lax-ass in his Sweet
drink." Mama, say Papa
where you come up
 with this stuff you be
thinking? I am not telling that
young man nothing!
Granddaddy start laughing
He, He, Ha, ha, ha! Granddaddy
said that ain't no young man
that's Cattail's doddle- boot-a.
Look at him Gal the next time

He run out the Shop. He be
trying to knock that 50 year
old Pine Tree down, Just to
get up in the house to the
toilet. One night he ran into
the Tree, I think he had
too much Corn liquor and
old! Lax-Ass passed out.
Grandmamma said lord help!
She said papa where do you
come up with a heap of
funny crazy stuff about
our customers here at
the cafe?

IN A STORM WITH YOU

You came in my
Life like a quiet
Storm.
We both swirl
around with each
other in thundering
Rain, we slip, slid
together and got
soapy wet.
we ran for cover
holding each other
arms into the bed
of a place like home.
As the quiet storm
started to break
a rush of wind
came in and blew
us away, you went
North and I went
South. As the wind
unwind us and
sent us separate
ways.
A common
feeling Lies within
me now days, when
a quiet storm come
rolling in where I
reside. I think of
of you, the love
and the laughter
we shared
in the storm.
wait for a rush
Wind to come in
and blow us back
together again.

GO SHARE YOUR GIFTS

This good girl thing is
driving me crazy.
I am about to give up
this celibacy stuff and
out right drop my
panties to the next
sexy sweet Brother
that looks like he
wants me and can hit
it. There is but so
much that a woman
can take, when her
hormones are flying
out of control. Now!
Being realist about
the nature of things,
Men and Women
were given Sexual
organs to share for
many reasons.
Hell!!!! When he
Comes I'm putting a
Glove on it and I'm
sharing my natural
gifts tonight, I
suggest you do the
same. Our gifts are
sensitive parts meant
to be shared, there
is no need to hold
your virginal hostage
ladies. Go on cover
it up, go Burn some
rubber with your,
little special
someone.
Seriously, get to

know a brother or
sister don't let loose
with no psycho's.
The world will
become more
beautiful when
you handle your
business. Mr. Right,
Ms. Right, the One!
will come soon as
they sees that after
glow on your faces
stiffing you out and
becoming a sexual
magnet. Grown Girls
go! Be carefully
share your gift, use
it before you lose it.

I LOVE YOU

I toss and turn with thoughts
of you in the day and in my bed
during the night.
I went over thousands of words in
my head, looking to define what
you mean to me.
I simply concluded with these
three words.
I love you.

CUT-IN JOSIE MAE AT CHURCH

Lord CUT-IN JOSIE Mae
came jumping out of
old Mr. Noney Old Car.
Lord, Grandma is looking
at her very hard.
Grandma said, "Lord she's
gonna be amess this
Sunday Morning, Rie!"
MY MA-Dear said," Yes,
Momma, she will be."
Lord, help her and us up
in that Church House.
They both shook their
heads. I said "Grandma
why you and Ma-Dear
is talking about
Cut-in Josie Mae."
They said at the same
time," please child,
you just be quiet and
gone up in the church
with the other little
children. I said"
Okay, I'll be sitting with
Cut-in Josie children."
Everyone had took
their seats and
positions in church.
The Preacher started
to preach, Amen and
yes Lord were heard
throughout the church.
We were singing and
rocking to the rhythms
of our Sweetwater,
Alabama Church.
Cut-in Josie started

singing loud and
clapping her hands.
Then she started
jumping around.
She were leaping in
The air then falling
on the floor with her
legs wide open in
front of the
Church members.
I think she forgot
She were wearing a
Dress, without a stich
of Bloomers and she
we're sitting facing the
Stage where all those
Men were. We all were
Lively in church. Cut-In
Josie-Mae were extra
Lively dancing and
sanging, like she doe's
Saturday Nights, at
Aunt El's Cafe.
Just before the chorus
finish singing, Cut-In
Josie-Mae caught a fit
and fell to the Floor
and start shaking
saying weird words
really fast with
her legs wide open.
Daddy," said
some folks get the,
"Holy Ghost." Daddy
said, he don't know
what the hell! Ms.
Josie Mae be getting.
Uncle Ben said,
"when they picked

Josie Mae up off the
Floor, carried her to
the back of the church,
to the cooling room.
She smelt a bit like
White lighting or
Corn Liquor, Daddy
said, he smelt it too.
Grand Momma and
Ma-dear said
they weren't
surprised, Cut-in
Josie Mae
was acting strange
in Church this Sunday.
They said, they hope
she cools off by next
Sunday. Ma-Dear
said, I told her not to
Marry that old man.
She's been out,
showing her ass ever
since she married
Old Man Noney.
 She want a
younger fella now.
Grandmamma said,
that's why she drink
so much and be
crawling around
Town with them other
Men like a Sneaky little
Cat. My Mu-Dear said,
Yes Lord!
Old man Noney can't
do a thang with her.
Ma-Dear said,
"Old Mr. Noney gone
tell the Preacher, her

Momma and Daddy.
She were drunk as
as a skunk, in Church
Sunday and that's
why she was leaping
like a bull frog!"
Josie Mae surely
not gonna like that.
My mother, cousins
and peers of
Josie Mae were
fill with Laughter
after Church was over.
They were over, on the
Church Lawn giggling,
Laughing at her until
tears were rolling down
their faces.
Cut-in Josie Mae walked
over with a Beautiful
Jazzy hat, gorgeous
Dress and nice shoes.
She said, what you
poor ass Mosquitos
are grinning and
laughing bout?
All yawl Mosquitos
Wish yawl had my Rich
old man Noney and
some White Lighting
this morning!
She strutted off to her
car. Cut-In Josie Mae is,
my Ma-dear first Cousin
on her Daddy side, they
grew up together like
most of everyone else
living in the Township.
Daddy said, "that

Josie Mae! Lord!
She done flipped
her wig. Lord, have
Mercy on Josie
she's the laugh of
the Town today.
After getting home
From Church
Grandma and
Ma-dear said,
We gonna sit on the
Porch and wave at her
and Mr. Noney when
they, pass by driving
5 minutes per miles.
Daddy said, look here
They're coming.
Grandma
and Ma-dear waved.
Daddy has a loud voice he
said, "Okay Now! "
Laughing He, He, Ha,
Ha, He!
What I mean! Both of
you have a nice evening.
Mr. Noney beeped his
Horn once and creeped
on down the road. Cut-in
Josie Mae wave like she
usually, do her hat
swallowed her face,
of shame.

MY MONEY JUG

Every time I think now days
I can't believe, I am not rich
with money.
My poor money jug is empty!
It used to be nearly full but now,
no Pennies, no Dimes, no Nickels,
no Quarters, no Fifty Cents and
no Dollar bills are in there. Money
never climbed up in my money jug
and got inside, I put it there. I just
can't believe my money is gone, the
jug is all clean out too! I know
my money Jug was not going get me
rich but dag! It being empty defines
me as being extra financially poor.
Dag!

LIQUID SUNSHINE

Liquid sunshine has
Came in today riding
high with the wind.
Them old wood tree
Branches are just
Dangling around out
there, filled with leaf
buds that are shedding.
The land is turning
green, Cherry Blossom
trees, grassy Green
Lawns and last year
flower beds are
coming back healthy
and strong. Melon
Vines and Fruit Trees
has come to a bloom.
Down the Red Dirt
Road where Liquid
Sunshine pours into
the River surrounded
by tree. Many creatures,
wild life, Live and creep
around out there. It is
a place where the
ancestors said, you can
smell the Earth before
Liquid Sunshine has
arrived and much better
after Liquid Sunshine
has come and gone.

MY PAYCHECK

I looked in my Pocketbook for my
Paycheck it was gone. It took me
two weeks to get a paycheck. I
look at the bills, I paid and
remembered, I cashed that check!
I paid my rent, insurance, Telephone
bill, bought a tank of gas, four bags
of grocery and my paycheck is gone!
I thought about my situation and
shook my Pocketbook on the kitchen
table what fell out were two dollars
and fifteen cent. I thought hard about
all my paydays past and future checks
to come, my head started to hurt, Yes,
it was high Blood Pressure! I said out
loud I work too hard to be broke and
living under poverty level with an every
two week Paydays. I shook, it was a
neurological disorder? I cried it was
depression coming in my life.
I laugh at me, because I were not about
claim no sickness or oppression because
I knew God gave me gifts. A voice rang
out in my Head repeatedly saying, "Did
you get paid? Did you get paid?
If you need a Paychecks then I suggest
you better Go get paid! "

POOR LITTLE GIRL NO, I DON'T KNOW

Poor little girl no,
I don't know.
Daddy and Mom
Gives her love they are
caring and supportive
Parents. They feed her,
clothes her, take her to
Church, School they
watch over her.
They taught her to
have respected for
herself and others.
Poor little girl no, I
don't know. She smile
a lot, running and
playing with her
Friends. She's full of
Life, laughter and joy.
She spreads love
everywhere, she goes.
She is so eager to
share her love and
happiness. Once she
amongst family, friends
and even strangers,
she gives her helping
hands. She shows her
bubbly, lovely, personality
 and shares her happiness.
All of those come in contact
with her are amazed by her
natural friendliness and
generosity. She loves people,
places and things.
A world she has only known for a
short time, she owns it. She
reaches out grasping the beauty

in everything and everyone in her
path. Her parents are just average
working parents with their moral
intact, their happy people. Some
would say their poor and their
Goddess daughter is a poor little
girl no, I don't know.
When talking about this little girl
and her parents, that is so far
from truth and cannot define
them. Poor little girl no, I don't
know. This little girl is living the
life all little children should be
living. When other little Children,
adults see her they embrace her
attitude and her kindness. She light
up rooms with her polite
mannerism and innocent charm.
Something about this little girl,
will brings back an adult childhood.
She bring natural happiness to the
Heart. She put a smile on faces.
That little happy girl is suppose
to be this way, let her Love and play.
Let's pray she blossom every day.
She's full of Love and happiness.
It is no doubt she's a flower with
remarkable beauty. She out there
caring, sharing, bringing Love and
happiness to others.
Poor little girl no, I don't Know.
Many people don't think so. That
little girl's is wealthy with a healthy
Mind and body. Poor little girl no, I
don't know, not that little girl.

TALES FROM BRONXDALE

NYCHA, Bronxdale Housing
use to be fill with joy you,
could look out the window
and see people in early morning
taking a scroll, children playing
in playground, basketball,
Football coming and going to
the supermarkets and elsewhere.
On weekends we had the early
Morning Party goers staggering
their way home young and old
some in crowd swearing loud.
Sunday's Morning was Church.
The people of Bronxdale were
so delightful and at peace
back then. Families knew each
other, fed family and friends.
The doors were open
welcoming those invited
to come in. No one here had
time to worry about what they
did not have, we were given
directives from family,
friends and community
Leaders and peace makers.
We grew up with the
abilities of knowing how
to get what we needed
and wanted. We were
taught to excel in school
achieve and be proud
of our accomplishments.
Friends were like your
family and all our elders
were respected. The
young were taught to
respect all elders and

disable.
We respected them like
our grandparent, parent,
Disable relatives we
saw no comparison they
was one of the same, being
disrespectful was outside
the norm in Bronxdale.
We also respected each
other. Police walked the
grounds here and they upheld
the law, us teenagers were
called by them "little ones."
We saw the police as big
and strong men wasn't
many women police back
then? The boys wanted
to be like police in
Bronxdale.
They advised us and saw
that we learn to behave,
we love them for that.
When we saw them we
would say Hey! Mr. Bill,
Hey! Mr. O'Connor.
They would say Hey little
ones! We felt like we
were someone Special,
they never had to
handcuff any of us. They
wouldn't have been able
to shake us out of
anything but Cigarettes
and quarts of beer if they
caught us. We would
never let them catch us
red handed with that
stuff, so we would hide
 our naughty little

crime. When we see them
heading our way. They were
a big part of our lives? We
did not want them to see us
behave badly. We also respect
our elder siblings we all had
our own special bench time.
In Bronxdale us teenagers had
go upstairs at six O'clock on
school nights we had to be
bench gone! ready to, eat
dinner, and take a bath and
go to bed. Months like April,
May and June it starts to get
warm or hot but for us it is
still School time, upstairs at
six week nights and weekend
at eight. When we went
upstairs the older Kids went
out to play mainly on those
warm nights. They would
be out there on our benches
singing and having a ball
with their cassette players.
Singing songs like doo
whoop my baby OO, ain't
Know mountain high
And 'know valley low enough,
Luis, Luis, Luis...,I'm your Mom,
I'm your Daddy, and I'm Your
Doctor when you need.
They were out laughing and
talking loud my sister belong
 to their group she would sit
with and party with them
when she were not studying
her college books but when
she was she did not want to
know them. They would sit

under our 7th floor
Window and start
singing late at night.
My sister would
say hey be quiet
out there! and go to
refrigerator and get
an egg and wait to
see if they continue
being loud, if
They did she would
through an egg
out the window near
them and tell them
go sit by your own
building where you all
live making that noise.
One boy had a Bass
Voice like one of the
Singers from the
Temptations R&B
Group, He said, yawl
better keep them
damn Eggs for breakfast
tomorrow girl.....!
My sister said, you all
be quiet. He started
singing, I can make it
rain whenever I want to
and the other boys join
in and said, ha, ha,
Ha-ha. My sister got up
filled two balloons
with water and threw
both out the window
on them and they got up
off the bench
running, saying Girl you
are crazy, we gone

get you tomorrow.
My sister said, you all
can make it rain
whenever you wanted it
to so look at you all are
wet. Ha, Ha, Ha, Ha....!
They said, damn! Girl you
crazy, you got us wet.
Bronxdale is my home,
memories of the good
times, I had living in
Bronxdale still bring me
laughter and joy.

TAKERS AND GIVERS CLUB

I hear them talking about
It, it's a place they want
me to come with them
and work.
They want you to come
too!
They say it's fun to see
those people that think
their on top of the world,
come tumbling down.
They say, "They don't like
them, they think
their better than other
People showing their
money and flexing their
muscles.
They say, come on down.
Hang with use let's
get acquainted, together
we'll take what they have.
We will take their material
things and bring them to
their knees.
They say if it's drugs their
seeking let's give it to
them, alcohol they want
let us pour it down their
Throats and smile with
them as they drink up,
if their looking for women
or Men for sex let us help,
 them get as much as they
like raw and nasty. We
don't care about if their
connecting partners are
dirty or clean we get
them and give them.

They say come on down
Join us, let's take what
they got.
If their mind are not on
their prizes our eyes and
minds will be, so come on
down you and join us, it's
The Takers and Givers
Club. It don't matter
where you from or what
you look like we have a
job for you. Once you
enter the Club doors you
are going to see how
they pay a price.
When you exit the doors
your pockets will be full
of cash and things. Your
Job was to assist, nothing
bad about your job you
are working at the Taker
and Givers Club!
Everything we offer is
what High Rollers and
Ballers are here and
ready for. When the
gig is over you'll be a
little dusty but you won't
be busted. Just brush
yourself off.
We will be waiting to see
you on your job again real
soon!

VISITING GRANDMA AND GRANDDAD

The kids leave to stay
with their grandparents
every summer.
When they return they sit
on the stoops and porches
with their friend and talk
about the fun they had on
their visit.
I use always like to talk
of Granddaddy. He's 88 but
If you ask him his age he's
Six---ty eight. Granddaddy
never want go to bed anymore
he just like sitting up looking.
Grandma yell for Granddaddy
to come bath mostly every night,
she said you going to be stinking
and you are not getting in any
beds in this House!" Granddaddy
say Okay Gal I'm coming.
Granddaddy is fussing he say,
hey Gal I'm coming but I done told
you ov-ber and ov-ber (over) again
a fish stay in the water all it life
and it still stinks they stank why
you want to keep me bathing every
night in that water. Grandma say,
man, go take a bath you ain't know
fish. Granddaddy say, you ain't know
spring Chicken either, Grandma says,
what that got to do with the prize of
Eggs. Granddaddy laughs He-he-
he-he. Okay Gal okay!

THINGS

If I knew you, I would give you things. I
would, I will give you things, I will chose
things you need and things you ask for
maybe, that's how I feel about things.
If you **want** things you should kindly put
in the work; get as many things you
want for the self they are only things.
I Don't worry much about too many
Damn things, they only things. We don't
need, many things. Things will weigh you
down. Things we have are not attached
to us. Thing are detached from us. Things
are not joining us in the **Afterlife.** Don't
take things to serious, things will stress
you out. Things have known, Know life.
Many things can help ruin our lives.
Just stay comfortable, survive!